PRAISE FOR CYNTHIA RYLANT'S
GOOSEBERRY PARK

★ "[A] rollicking animal tale. . . . Readers will relish every moment of this impeccably paced fantasy and its winning depictions of the unique perspectives and quandaries of four unlikely companions."
—*Publishers Weekly*, starred review

"In a humorous contemporary fable about friendship, courage, and loyalty, Rylant creates an unlikely trio of friends: Stumpy, a red squirrel, Kona, a Labrador . . . and Murray, a dumpster-scavenging bat with a fondness for egg rolls. . . . It's a simple story, but the tongue-in-cheek humor is sophisticated and funny."
—*Kirkus Reviews*

"Howard's liberally distributed illustrations are hysterical, as are Rylant's descriptions and dialogue. Confident readers will want to race through this delightful tale, whereas those less facile will relish a nightly chapter."
—*Family Fun*

O9-AIC-482

Nash

Other books by Cynthia Rylant

Missing May
The Heavenly Village
The Van Gogh Cafe

Cynthia Rylant
Gooseberry Park

ILLUSTRATED BY ARTHUR HOWARD

SCHOLASTIC INC.
New York Toronto London Auckland Sydney
Mexico City New Delhi Hong Kong Buenos Aires

Thank you, AJ and DP

If you purchased this book without a cover, you should be aware that this book is stolen property. It was reported as "unsold and destroyed" to the publisher, and neither the author nor the publisher has received any payment for this "stripped book."

No part of this publication may be reproduced, stored in a retrieval system, or transmitted in any form or by any means, electronic, mechanical, photocopying, recording, or otherwise, without written permission of the publisher. For information regarding permission, write to Harcourt, Inc., 6277 Sea Harbor Drive, Orlando, FL 32887-6777.

ISBN 0-590-94715-X

Text copyright © 1995 by Cynthia Rylant.
Illustrations copyright © 1995 by Arthur Howard. All rights reserved. Published by Scholastic Inc., 557 Broadway, New York, NY 10012, by arrangement with Harcourt, Inc. SCHOLASTIC, APPLE PAPERBACKS, and associated logos are trademarks and/or registered trademarks of Scholastic Inc.

12 11 10 9 8 7 6 5 4 3   4 5 6 7 8 9/0

Printed in the U.S.A.   40

To Caitlyn Cushner and Kona

Contents

Contents

Gooseberry
Park

CHAPTER ONE

A New Nest

All new mothers have a nesting instinct, even human mothers who haven't any idea how to build a nest.

While human mothers are waiting for their babies to be born, their nesting instinct causes them to do the silliest things, such as taking all the pots out of one cabinet and all the pans out of another and switching them. Human mothers don't know why they are doing this except that some little voice in their heads is saying "Keep busy! Keep busy!"

A sensible *rabbit* mother who hears this little voice will simply pluck her fur with her teeth to make a nice warm baby bed for the near future. But a mixed-up human mother will just wander about her kitchen, switching her cabinets for no reason at all.

Thus it was a good thing that Stumpy was a squirrel. She knew a nesting instinct when she felt one, and she knew what to do about it.

For many days now, every part of her red squirrel body had been shouting "Keep busy! Keep busy!" And was she ever keeping busy! For the new nest she was building, she had collected the choicest twigs and the finest leaves and—because she was

A New Nest

sure of what was about to happen—bits of the pink-dotted, blue-flowered, or green-starred material that could be had by a little digging in the can behind the town sewing shop. One morning she had even happened upon a bit of cloth decorated with pictures of little red squirrels carrying small, brown nut sacks, and she nearly fainted away. It was better than she could have hoped for her new babies.

And new babies indeed were what she was about to have. Babies to love, to keep clean, to bring up close against her fur in the dark night. Stumpy was about to become a mother and, oh, was she proud.

And busy. Quite busy.

Carefully she lined her new nest with the twigs, the leaves, and the bits of beautiful cloth. She had recently moved from an old locust tree on the south side of Gooseberry Park to a pin oak on the east. She had moved because, like most who live alone, Stumpy had been rather relaxed about her housekeeping, and her old nest had become difficult to move around in. You see, Stumpy was a collector, and her nest was full of treasures. She had tremendous energy, and after she had found as many acorns and pinecones as could be eaten by one little squirrel, she burned up the rest of her energy by collecting.

Stumpy collected these things:

> tabs from soda pop cans
> empty yogurt cups
> gum wrappers
> coins
> ice-cream sticks
> straws
> feathers
> pretty pebbles
> little balls lost by children
> nuts, bolts, screws, tacks
> twist ties
> rubber bands

Her most beautiful treasure of all, though, had been a lovely watch that glowed in the dark. Two winters ago, she had found it lying on top of a picnic table. She took it to her nest and didn't realize until

A New Nest

evening what a marvel it was. As darkness came, the watch began to shine and Stumpy's nest became bathed in a soft green light. Animals who passed at night were drawn to it. Everyone came to see it. And news spread far and wide of the glow-in-the-dark nest in Gooseberry Park.

A New Nest

Unfortunately, the news spread too far and too wide. Someone came one day and stole that watch from Stumpy's nest. Stumpy never found it again, though for weeks she sat high in her tree at night and looked out over the park, hoping to see that soft green glow.

She never did.

Still, Stumpy had other treasures. In fact, too many treasures, and her collection had gotten all out of control. Stumpy knew that no self-respecting mother of several young children could have her babies sleeping among wood screws and twist ties.

So she found a new tree and built a clean nest and organized her collection to give plenty of room for her babies. Her friend Kona would be proud of her housecleaning. Each time she collected something new, Kona would say to her:

"Stump, you've too many things."

And she would answer, "Not things. Treasure."

And Kona would say, "Stump, my owner Professor Albert has a chess set crafted in pure silver. A crystal punch bowl. And a set of Limoges china. *That's* treasure."

A New Nest

Well, what could a Labrador dog know about treasure anyway, thought Stumpy. Kona was a good friend, a fine friend. But he had no imagination. If he had, he'd be living in the park collecting feathers and balls instead of sitting in a boring ranch house with Professor Albert.

Stumpy had babies and copper pennies and even the chance of finding another glow-in-the-dark watch to look forward to. She went on carefully layering her maple leaves and flowered cloth and green twigs into a safe, warm pocket.

Her friend Kona might not regard gum wrappers and ice-cream sticks as treasure. But Stumpy knew the noble dog would not mistake the priceless value of new life in the tall pin oak tree. The tree that for her would be a harbor in a storm. The tree that her own babies would call home.

CHAPTER TWO

Night Talk

"Gwendolyn, are you awake?"

The dog pushed his nose up against the clear glass bowl and looked inside, cross-eyed. It was a cloudy night, and only the warm glow of the gas lamp outside the window gave any light to the room. The Labrador concentrated his attention on the glistening shell lying in the bowl.

"Gwendolyn?"

Scritch. Scrape.

Gwendolyn slowly turned herself around and put

her hermit crab head out to meet the large dark eyes staring in.

"Lovely evening, isn't it, Kona? And nearly a full moon. I can feel it in my bones."

"You have no bones, Gwendolyn," said the Labrador.

"Figure of speech, dear, figure of speech. I expect it's simply the memory of a time when I did. Perhaps I had even more bones than usual. I may have been a hawk in a previous life. Hawks are nothing but bone, I hear."

"Have you been watching public television with Professor Albert again?"

"Well," the old crab said, smiling, *"Amazing Birds of Prey,* if you must know. Personally I'd rather be all tucked up and dreaming of the sea. But Professor Albert is such a dear, and he does love the company."

"I take him to the park," said Kona. "I try to give him company, too."

"You try at everything you do, dear Kona," Gwendolyn answered. "That is why I like you so."

Kona wagged his tail proudly.

Night Talk

"I have some news for you, Gwendolyn," he said.

"Wonderful."

"First, tomorrow should be a high of fifty-two degrees and partly sunny."

"Excellent," said the crab. "So kind of you to watch the evening weather report while I'm napping, dear. So kind. Oh, I do love the weather. I am nearly certain I was a sheep in a past life. Sheep are very weather sensitive, you know."

"I didn't know," said Kona. "And guess what else, Gwendolyn."

Night Talk

"Sunrise at six o'clock," said the crab.

"No," said Kona. "Babies."

"Babies at six o'clock?"

"Oh no, just babies," answered the dog. *"Real* babies. Well, not real babies like dog babies. Real babies like *squirrel* babies. Stumpy Squirrel is expecting!"

"You don't say!" answered Gwendolyn.

"Any day now," added Kona.

"Lovely," said Gwendolyn.

"She's building a new nest in a pin oak on the east side of Gooseberry Park. And she's organizing her collection."

"How exciting," said the crab.

"She's dashing about like I've never seen her dash before," Kona continued. "And you know how Stumpy can dash."

"I do," said Gwendolyn. "You've mentioned it many times."

"Yes, I suppose I have," Kona answered. "Every time I see her now, she's running in circles with a mouthful of rubber bands or ice-cream sticks or maple leaves. . . ."

Night Talk

"The nesting instinct," said Gwendolyn, waving a claw in the air. "Happens every time."

Gwendolyn explained to Kona all about the nesting instinct, and as the night lengthened, the two friends talked on. Kona was glad to have Gwendolyn share his excitement about Stumpy's new babies. Kona's favorite animals were squirrels and hermit crabs. He wasn't terribly fond of dogs, though. Dogs could be rude and loud. And leave it to a dog to tell *everyone* your secrets. Squirrels never told secrets. Nor did hermit crabs, especially ones who had been reincarnated seventeen times.

Gwendolyn let Kona dream aloud about the prospect of being an uncle. She smiled with affection as he explained the way he thought young squirrels should be raised. She laughed when he predicted he'd have the children catching a Frisbee between their teeth by July.

Babies were on the way, and it was exciting.

CHAPTER THREE

Friends

Kona had been born in the family room of a fifth-grade teacher on Paradise Lane, Stumpy had been born in a sugar maple near the south entrance of Gooseberry Park, and Gwendolyn had been born in a palm tree on an island somewhere in the Caribbean. It was a miracle that the three had ever found each other.

Of course, this was mostly Professor Albert's doing. He was a retired biology professor who loved to grow daylilies and listen to the saxophone.

Friends

Professor Albert had never married, liked living alone, and all the years he was a professor he never minded the fact that he had no family. He was too busy teaching the cell structures of amphibians.

But after he retired and found himself home so much of the time, he began to grow a little lonely. And when he started talking back to the radio ("Oh yes, *I* love outpatient care, too!"), he realized he needed a pet.

So he bought himself a hermit crab. She was the loveliest of all the crabs in the pet store. Her shell was creamy white with wavy brown lines flowing across it. She was quite big—twice the size of the other crabs—and Professor Albert found her enchanting. So he brought her home from the store in a little paper box, named her Gwendolyn, and became her friend.

Gwendolyn turned out to be a wonderful companion. Professor Albert carried her bowl from room to room in the house, depending on what needed doing. If he was in the kitchen baking banana bread, Gwendolyn was on the kitchen counter. If he was in

Friends

the living room watching television, Gwendolyn was on the coffee table. If he was writing letters in his study, Gwendolyn was on the desk.

Professor Albert knew that Gwendolyn liked him because she always pulled her head far up out of her shell to look at him when he talked to her. ("Gwendolyn, did you know that each giraffe's markings are unique?") As the professor spoke, Gwendolyn's delicate antennae moved gracefully back and forth, and he knew she was listening carefully (having been a teacher, he was quite good at picking out careful listeners). It was nice, having her.

Friends

Professor Albert was very happy with his hermit crab and he had no plans at all to get a dog. He didn't know he needed a dog. He had never even thought about it.

But one day one of his neighbors who had a sister who had a son in the fifth-grade class of a woman who lived on Paradise Lane told Professor Albert about the teacher's brand-new litter of puppies. Twelve in all. Twelve! The professor could not imagine so many puppies. He tried imagining twelve hermit crabs. So many bowls to carry! How did anyone manage twelve puppies?

His neighbor said that the puppies were chocolate Labradors. Chocolate Labradors! The professor imagined children finding these instead of chocolate rabbits in their Easter baskets. The neighbor said the puppies were round like beach balls and that they loved to play. They played and played and played.

And when Professor Albert heard this, something lit up inside him. Something from when he was a boy. It had to do with dogs and playing.

And before he knew it he was telling his neighbor, "I would like to have one of those puppies."

So Professor Albert found himself in the family room of a fifth-grade teacher on Paradise Lane with twelve fat little puppies running all over him and all over each other and all over everything else in the room. He was delighted and overwhelmed and could hardly catch his breath, and he wondered how he would ever choose just one puppy from so many. They all looked pretty much the same. Should he just pick one up and go?

Friends

But as he was trying to figure all of this out, one of the happy puppies crawled into his lap and stayed. It stayed and stayed and stayed. The other puppies romped across him, licked his face, then ran off somewhere else. But this puppy stayed.

The fifth-grade teacher said to Professor Albert, "Of them all, that's the one who likes to be held the most. He likes company. He'll be glad when he's the only puppy somewhere."

Professor Albert smiled. He knew all about liking company. And this little puppy was staying.

He took the puppy home. He named him Kona, after his favorite coffee. And there in that house Kona grew up.

Friends

Of course, Gwendolyn and Kona became best friends right away. Though Professor Albert couldn't understand Gwendolyn's language, Kona could, and very quickly Gwendolyn assumed the job of puppy training.

"No, Kona dear, you are not allowed to chew Professor Albert's slippers."

"No, Kona dear, dogs do not eat encyclopedias."

"No, Kona dear, you must wait until you are outside to do that. Do you want to go outside? Then sit at the door and bark for Professor Albert. That's right. Bark!"

Kona did everything Gwendolyn told him to do, and Professor Albert said to everyone that raising a puppy was the easiest job in the world. This amused Gwendolyn very much.

Friends

It was a few years more before Kona met the little red squirrel called Stumpy. Gooseberry Park was a very large park with many trees and many more squirrels, and to Kona, of course, all of the squirrels looked alike. Kona went to the park every day with Professor Albert, and while the professor read books about snails and baboons and ants and lilies, listening to Charlie Parker on his Walkman, Kona explored the park and ignored the squirrels.

Then one day as he was exploring, Kona came upon a little red squirrel who was trying to pull a plastic toy tractor up a tree. Holding the tractor in her teeth, the little squirrel pulled it halfway up the tree trunk. But the tractor slipped and crashed to the ground. She ran down to the bottom to start all over again.

Kona walked over to speak to her.

"Perhaps if you pushed it . . . ," he suggested, as the squirrel began pulling at the tractor yet again.

The squirrel opened her mouth. "What?" The tractor crashed.

"Oops," said Kona. "Sorry."

Friends

The little squirrel ran down to try once more.

"It's for my collection," she said to the dog. "I haven't anything this big. Do you know what it's called?"

"A tractor. I've seen them on television," Kona answered.

"Television?" asked the squirrel.

Kona sometimes forgot the world really did have wild animals in it. He couldn't imagine anyone not knowing what a television was.

"Never mind," said Kona. "I simply suggested you push it. Put your paws on the back and roll it up the tree. Just like a boy would."

"Good idea!" said the squirrel. And she pushed the toy tractor all the way up the tree trunk and into her nest. She disappeared inside and was gone for several minutes. Kona started to walk away.

"I'm Stumpy!" The squirrel's little red head popped out of her nest just as the dog was leaving.

"I'm Kona," called the Labrador, happily turning back. "What else do you collect?"

Friends

And that is how Kona met Stumpy. He visited her tree every time Professor Albert took a park bench nap—which was quite often—and from Stumpy he heard tales of life in Gooseberry Park, which he reported back to Gwendolyn, who commented on them as most elderly animals will:

"Leave it to a raccoon to make a mess of things!"

"Oh yes indeed, crows are quite the smart alecks."

"There's nothing like a young possum to warm the heart."

"Thank goodness for rabbits."

These comments Kona took back to Stumpy, and in this way they all became friends.

It was a fine life. A life just right for babies.

CHAPTER FOUR

Murray

It was her first night in her lovely, clean, new nest. Stumpy slept peacefully, feeling the babies move inside her. What a perfectly peaceful . . .

"OUCH!"

Stumpy jumped. Was she dreaming or had someone just yelled "Ouch"? She lay very still and listened. Someone else was definitely in her tree. There was rattling and stumbling above her. Twigs were falling all around. Her first night in the new tree, and here had come a noisy neighbor.

"EXCUSE ME!" yelled Stumpy irritably.

Silence.

"What?" someone called back.

"I said, *'Excuse me,'* " called Stumpy.

"Oh, no problem."

Silence.

"Wait a minute," called the voice. "Was that *sarcasm?*"

Stumpy frowned.

"I'm just trying to get a little sleep here because my babies—"

"BABIES?"

There came a *flum-flum-flum*. Suddenly, perched

on the edge of Stumpy's nest was a tiny black-and-silver bat. He was grinning broadly.

"I *love* babies," he said. He shook Stumpy's paw and peered into her nest.

"So where are they?"

Stumpy, by now, was speechless. Here was a bat in her home in the middle of the night, chatting. She couldn't find her voice, so she simply pointed to her stomach.

"You ate your babies?" asked the bat.

"Who *are* you?" Stumpy finally managed to ask.

The bat grinned and shook Stumpy's paw again.

"Murray," he said. "Name's Murray. And you?"

"Stumpy."

"Pleased to meet you," said the bat. "Did you just move in?"

Stumpy nodded.

"Hey!" Murray said with great cheer. "We'll be neighbors. I've tried every tree in East Gooseberry, and this is the only one that doesn't have a woodpecker living in it. Talk about ruining a neighborhood. Just *you* try to sleep while a woodpecker's having breakfast.

"Speaking of food," said the bat, "have you eaten? Want to go out for Chinese? There's this big green Dumpster over on Sixth that's always full of egg rolls and tasty little packages of duck sauce. Well, tasty if you're not a duck. So, want to go?"

Stumpy looked carefully at the bat.

"You're nocturnal, aren't you?" she asked.

"No way," said Murray. "I'm a Democrat."

"No, no," said Stumpy. "Nocturnal means you sleep all day and stay up all night."

"I knew that," said Murray.

"So?" asked Stumpy.

Murray seemed confused. Then he remembered the question.

"Oh!" he said with relief. "Oh yes. I'm as nocturnal as they come. Do you want to go for Chinese or not?"

Stumpy was very big, very heavy with babies, and also very tired. And she was not nocturnal. She thought it best to stay home. So instead, she invited Murray in for a bite of fresh pita bread she'd found that morning.

Murray

In spite of the rude awakening, Stumpy was happy for Murray's company. She sensed that her babies were due to arrive very soon, and it was good having him to talk to. She didn't feel lonely or afraid. Murray told her all about his cousin Rudy's sinus problems and his great-aunt Miriam's bad knee and the heart palpitations that ran in his family.

He also told her about the fall he'd had as a young bat, when he was hanging from a tree by one foot and trying to unwrap a Mars bar with the other. He had gotten so excited that he slipped and hit the ground headfirst. Since then he'd had some problems with his echolocation and couldn't seem to fly in the dark without bumping into things.

Murray

"You'd think I'd manage not to bump into my own tree," said Murray sheepishly. "But I do. All the time."

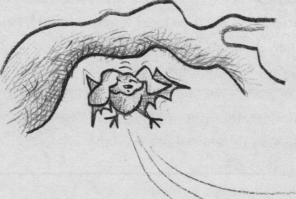

"How long have you lived in Gooseberry Park?" asked Stumpy.

"Oh, all my life," said Murray. "I was born on the North Side into a big family. Four girls and a boy. My sisters are crazy about music, so they moved into town over a store called the Vinyl Nightmare. And my parents retired to Disneyland. They're living in one of those houses in It's a Small World. So now it's just me. I tried to fix the old place up after my folks left, but it was too big a job. Lots of shag car-

28

peting. My mother loved shag carpet. In our living room—"

"You had a living room?" asked Stumpy.

"Oh sure," said Murray. "It was a split-level. And how about you?"

"Well, I collect things," said Stumpy.

"Yeah?"

"Yes, I—OH!" Stumpy grabbed her stomach.

"Pardon?" Murray said.

"OH!" Stumpy cried out again.

Murray's eyes grew large.

"Indigestion?" he asked. ". . . Or babies?"

"I think I need to be alone now," Stumpy said, still holding her stomach.

Murray jumped up.

"Absolutely!" he said. "I've got a million things to do anyway. Empty the garbage, water my plants, floss. I am *out* of here."

He perched on the edge of the nest, then looked back at Stumpy, worried.

"If you need me, just yell. I'm only one flight up."

Stumpy smiled.

"Good night, Murray. I'll be fine. I'll call you in the morning."

The tiny bat grinned.

"Babies!" he said. Then he was gone.

Alone, Stumpy swept away the remaining pita crumbs, then curled herself into a warm corner of the nest where she had made a special bed of sweet-smelling pine needles. She closed her eyes and took several deep breaths.

"So how many ducks do you think it *takes* to make one of those little packages of sauce?" called a voice from above.

Stumpy smiled.

CHAPTER FIVE

Time

"Kona," Gwendolyn whispered into the darkness. "It's begun."

The dog lifted his large brown head from his bed in the corner of the living room.

"Listen," said Gwendolyn.

Kona held himself quite still and listened. There was the ticking of the Swiss clock on the mantel. The hush of warm air from the gas fireplace. The subtle buzz of the plant light above Professor Albert's violets. And . . . something else.

Time

"Can you feel it in the air, Kona?" Gwendolyn shifted her shell around to look at him directly.

Kona waited, and as he did, a most powerful feeling came over him.

"Is it Stumpy?" he whispered. "Is it time?"

The old crab stretched her antennae as high as they could reach. She searched the air.

"I believe it is time," she said with conviction.

Oh." Kona jumped up. "Oh."

He went to the picture window and looked out toward the tops of the trees in Gooseberry Park.

"I wish I could be there," he said. He rested his front paws upon the windowsill.

"Kona dear," said Gwendolyn, "you are a most remarkable dog. But, I am sorry to say, not so remarkable as to climb a tree and assist a squirrel having babies."

"I wish I were," Kona said with a sigh. "I wish I were that remarkable."

"She'll be fine, dear," Gwendolyn said reassuringly, fully believing this herself. "She's a plucky one."

Kona stared out toward the park a while longer,

then he began to pace. He went from the living room to the dining room, turned right at the sideboard to the study, circled the study, then paced back to the living room exactly the way he'd come. He longed for a good bone to chew, but he'd left his best one in the backyard. He plopped down on the floor and began chewing the leg of the coffee table.

"Kona!" yelled Gwendolyn.

"What?!" The dog jumped so fast that he banged

his nose on the table. "Thanks, Gwendolyn. Forgot where I was. I don't think there's much damage."

The old crab shook her head.

"Kona, my dear, there are some things in this life we must experience alone."

"Even having babies?" asked Kona.

"Even having babies," answered Gwendolyn. "Why, when I had my children—"

"Gwendolyn, *you* have children?" Kona's eyes were wide with surprise.

The crab smiled.

"Dear, I had quite a full life in the tropics before I was carried off to be sold in a pet shop. Not that I'm complaining, mind you. I am very devoted to our Professor Albert."

Time

"Children?" asked Kona.

"At least fifty," answered Gwendolyn. "All grown now. And let me tell you, my friend, giving birth is something very private, and rather sacred. It was, for me, as private as prayer."

"Oh," said Kona with a solemn look on his face.

Together the two gazed out the window in silence, at the trees, the stars, the clear bright moon in the sky. Each was full of thoughts: thoughts about the earth and its heavens, about mothers and their children, about the profound comfort of shelter and sustenance and the familiarity of home. And both sent forth their best, their strongest, their most sustaining thoughts to a little red squirrel who, at that very moment, was happily nursing two baby boys and one baby girl in the good green fragrance of a pin oak tree.

CHAPTER SIX

Children

The following several days were rather heady ones for the little red squirrel who had become a mother. Never had she received so much attention and praise. Never had she been so talked about. The birth of new babies is important news anywhere, and Gooseberry Park was no exception. Word spread quickly through the trees and burrows and along the riverbank that triplets had been born to the busy red squirrel who collected yogurt cups. Friends Stumpy hadn't seen in months suddenly dropped by, carrying gifts of hard, pungent walnuts or choice bits of ham sandwich or the occasional french fry, which was considered quite a delicacy in park circles. Red, gray, and black squirrels oohed and aahed. Mourning doves cooed, starlings cackled, and cardinals peeked shyly over the edge of the nest. Even a fat old possum hoisted himself up the tree to pay his respects.

A brisk, cold wind was blowing now, unusual for early April. The park was strangely quiet as the trees leaned into the chilly breezes. But Stumpy had no worries. She had three beautiful babies, a fine collection of treasures, and a wonderful new neighbor who loved bringing her egg rolls. The winds could blow as hard as they might. She was secure.

Kona, of course, had been by to visit every day since the babies' arrival. He still hadn't met Murray, since the bat slept most of the day. And, of course, Kona hadn't met Stumpy's children yet, either. They were much too tiny to be carried down to the ground. But Stumpy herself came down when Kona called her name, and she told him all the wonderful details. She said the little girl loved to sleep and that she sang in her sleep like a little bird. The two baby boy squirrels liked to rest on each other, and one preferred the bottom and one preferred the top, so she had named them Top and Bottom. The little girl was called Sparrow for her pretty songs. Their eyes weren't even open yet.

Stumpy said it was hard work, being a mother to newborns. She couldn't waste time or explore for fun anymore. Whenever she left the nest, it was only to pull a few pinecones from a tree stump or to unearth a few acorns buried nearby. Then she had to hurry back home, for her babies would be waking and crying to be fed. She had never felt so needed. She had never felt so tired.

Children

Still, she told Kona, she had never felt so happy. And Murray visited every night.

Kona trotted cheerfully back home and reported to Gwendolyn, word for word, everything Stumpy had told him. Though Gwendolyn had never met Stumpy personally, she regarded the squirrel as an old friend, and she was glad for the good news from Kona. Glad for the babies in Gooseberry Park.

CHAPTER SEVEN

Ice

New babies alone cannot change the designs of fate, and no one knew, not even Gwendolyn, the drama that lay just ahead for Stumpy and for all of the animals in Gooseberry Park. The park had known its share of danger. The animals had lived through drought and the specter of a dying river. They had watched a tornado take a few trees from the South Side one spring. There had been deep snow and lightning and the threat of a boy with an air rifle.

I c e

But what they were about to face was a danger none of them could have imagined.

When just before dawn the freezing rain began to fall, Gwendolyn, looking out Professor Albert's window, knew that a day of trouble had arrived. Morning came, and the steady *pick pick pick* of icy pellets against the house kept Professor Albert and Kona and Gwendolyn at the window, their faces full of concern. And as the day wore on and the ice thickened, the earth all around them began to suffer.

Ice dropped from the sky and covered everything. It coated houses, swing sets, streetlights, telephone wires. It encased picnic tables, cars, fences, trains. And it froze trees. The trees were first wet and cold and slick. Then the slickness hardened and became ice. And the ice grew thicker and thicker and heavier and heavier, and soon the trees began to bow their weary limbs until finally the limbs snapped, crashing to the ground. The sap froze in other trees and exploded with a sound like gunpowder as they fell.

Professor Albert had just planted a pink dogwood and a small flowering crab apple and a gingko tree.

I c e

All three were too young to withstand the assault of the ice, and during the course of the afternoon they dropped, one by one. Professor Albert had tried to run out and throw a quilt over the gingko, but he fell down his front steps and slid all the way to the mailbox. Kona stood at the door and barked and barked.

The professor hobbled back into his house, muttering that he should have moved to Florida with all of the other retired professors. He fixed himself a cup of hot Darjeeling tea, then, and, sore and exhausted, promptly went to sleep. He slept so soundly, tucked under a knitted throw on his living room sofa, that even the loudest snap of falling branches didn't stir him. Kona and Gwendolyn were left to do all of the worrying.

And, of course, it was not the fate of gingko trees that had them knotted up inside. It was the fate of their small squirrel friend and her newborn children.

No one could have guessed which trees in Gooseberry Park would stand through the storm and which trees would fall. No one could have guessed that an old ash tree over by the river would bend and groan and suffer under the weight of the ice, but would hold steady. And that other stronger, sturdier trees —oak trees—would break.

When the storm began, Stumpy had burrowed herself and her babies under the thick blanket of twigs and leaves in her nest to keep dry, as she always did in a rain. And when the rain had become ice, persistently tapping against the leaf blanket, still Stumpy had not been afraid. She had endured sleet, and a little fine ice on the trees was no worry to her.

Ice

But when the leaf blanket grew heavier and heavier with its freezing weight, and a deep, cold chill that she could not warm began to run through Stumpy's body, and as the air filled with the groans and agonizing cracks of trees falling under, the little red squirrel became very, very afraid. Had she been alone, she would have fled her nest and gone to a safe underground burrow.

But Stumpy was not alone. She had three babies, babies whose eyes were barely open and whose bodies were still pink in places where the fur had not yet grown in, babies who could not be moved in a deluge of icy rain without great risk.

Stumpy drew the three babies more tightly under her body and tried to calm their whimperings each time a dying tree cracked like thunder on its way down. She wondered how Murray was, if he was as frightened as she, if he also was wishing for the comfort of company. Under the weight of the ice, she could not call to him. She hoped he was safe wherever he was, and she tried to cheer herself up by imagining him trapped in the Chinese Dumpster, under the ice with a week's worth of egg rolls. And it was when she was thinking of him, and smiling to herself, that a kind of explosion sounded in her ears, and her world lost its balance and went falling, falling to the cold, hard ground.

CHAPTER EIGHT

A Very Big Risk

When evening descended and the ice storm had stopped, the professor still slept while Kona kept vigil at the window, trembling as giant pines bent their icy heads to the ground and jumping at the sharp sounds of thick bark breaking. All of the lights in the neighborhood were out. The refrigerator didn't hum, the plant light didn't buzz, and the warm furnace air didn't hush through the vents. Professor Albert's fireplace and the gas post lamp in the front yard were the only sources of light, and they cast a funereal glow upon the house and its occupants, stranded like polar bears on an arctic floe.

A Very Big Risk

"What are we going to do, Gwendolyn?" Kona asked, his big head casting a giant shadow over her bowl. "Stumpy is in serious trouble."

"Yes," Gwendolyn answered, nodding. "It's serious, very serious. Even if her tree is still standing, she will be trapped in her nest. And the ice . . . the babies . . ."

"I have to help her," Kona said, pacing in circles around the living room.

"Kona dear, what can you do? She is at the top of a tall tree. There would be no way of reaching her. And the journey to the park—treacherous, very treacherous indeed. The ice is difficult—nearly impossible—to cross, as poor Professor Albert demonstrated earlier. Trees are coming down, heavy branches dropping from great heights. Kona, you would be taking a very big risk. And perhaps for naught. She is over a hundred feet in the air."

"What if she isn't, Gwendolyn?" Kona stopped pacing and looked at the crab. "What if her tree is one of those that came down?"

Gwendolyn shook her head sadly.

A Very Big Risk

"If it was, then I very much doubt, dear, that Stumpy . . . such a fall . . ."

The old crab looked at the dog and spoke gently, "Her chance of surviving seems very unlikely."

Kona took a deep breath and, with eyes wide and sincere, answered, "Whether she is alive or not, Gwendolyn, I have to take care of her."

The crab sighed.

"Well, my dear, I expect you do, I expect you do. But I am not sure how you will accomplish it."

Five minutes later, Gwendolyn was working the lock on Professor Albert's front door.

A Very Big Risk

Kona held her steadily in his mouth, and with a deft claw she turned the mechanism gently, gently, then *click.* It was done.

Kona placed her back in her bowl.

"Thank you for not sneezing, dear," she said.

"I'm still not sure if I can get the door open," said Kona.

"Just pretend the knob is a bone," Gwendolyn answered. "I have every confidence you will do it."

And the dog did. After only a minute or so of vigorous gnawing and biting, the door popped open.

A Very Big Risk

Kona looked back at his good friend staring anxiously through the glass, at Professor Albert snoring peacefully on the sofa, at his own warm bed in the corner, and at the inviting flames of the fireplace.

"I'll be back soon, Gwendolyn," he said.

"Of course you will," said the crab. "Take good care, dear." She did not want Kona to know how worried she was.

When Kona went out the front door, he didn't close it all the way behind him. He needed to be able to get back into the house before Professor Albert woke again. Kona breathed deeply, took one strong, confident step, and with a magnificent slide, shot right off Professor Albert's porch into the top of a juniper bush.

Sprawled there, he groaned and looked out at the several blocks he would have to cross to reach Gooseberry Park. He looked back at Gwendolyn in the window, her antennae swirling around and around. Just then a heavy branch from a tree across the street crashed into his neighbor's front yard, taking several broken shingles with it.

A Very Big Risk

Kona sighed, then carefully maneuvered back onto his feet. Inching his way slowly, he began his icy journey. Gooseberry Park seemed to him to be on the other side of the world.

Instead of taking the sidewalk, Kona decided to cut through yards. It would save time, and there would be more things to hold on to. He crossed one yard by hanging on to a hemlock hedge. A second yard had a rail fence he steadied himself against. In another, a long concrete planter kept him on his feet.

Some yards had nothing at all to hold on to except the occasional ice-covered bush. In these yards Kona danced, skated, skied, and rolled. He fell again and again, and once he struck his nose so hard that it bled. Kona saw not one sign of life along the way, save

A Very Big Risk

for a large yellow tomcat who tried to impress him by strolling easily across the icy top of an Oldsmobile. Kona gave him a sour look and went on.

The dog's body was bruised and his spirits had taken a beating as well, but he was determined. He knew where to find Stumpy's tree and he was bound to make it there. Something inside was telling him to do this. His teeth ached from holding on to every solid object he could grasp, and his tongue was numb with cold.

But something called him. And no matter the price, he would answer.

CHAPTER NINE

Rescue and Remorse

When he finally reached Stumpy's pin oak tree, Kona was stunned by what he saw. The top of the tree had been snapped off like a bean. What was left of its lower trunk still stood sharp and upright, ice hanging down its sides like a fresh-cut wound. Scattered across the ground lay the debris that had once given the giant oak its majesty: solid pieces of trunk, mammoth branches with long, graceful stems, hundreds of broken twigs—all glistening under a hard layer of ice. Kona could barely breathe.

Rescue and Remorse

For a moment he simply closed his eyes.

Then he whispered, "Stumpy?"

His voice was lost in the desolation of the park.

He cleared his throat and this time spoke louder, "Stumpy?"

Clamping his teeth on to the scattered branches to steady himself, he made his way around what was left of the tree. Every few feet he called out "Stumpy?" Each time he was met by silence. And when he found a part of Stumpy's nest scattered on the ground, bits of bright material and gum wrappers thrown everywhere, it was almost more than he could bear. He sat down and hung his head.

Rescue and Remorse

Stopped there, motionless, discouraged, confused, and very cold, Kona heard a sound. It was a sound like a song. He lifted his ears. The sound was coming from within a large piece of broken trunk that had rolled away from the rest of the debris and settled against a broad rhododendron bush. Kona stood up and listened more intently.

"Rock-a-bye Bottom in the tree Top!" someone sang. "Get it?"

"Stump!" Kona's voice boomed across the wreckage. "Stump!"

The dog leaped forward then danced like a Bolshevik until he landed beside the singing tree trunk, flat on his back. He moaned. From a small round hole in the trunk, a little black head fuzzed with silver poked out. It looked at Kona.

"Help!" the head shouted.

Kona raised himself up and moved closer. The little black head that had yelled for help belonged to a bat.

"Murray?" he inquired.

"In person!" answered the bat.

"Are you all right?" Kona asked.

"I think we bounced," said Murray. "You must be

Kona. I knew Stumpy would find you. The kids are all in here, snoring like elephants."

"Stumpy didn't find me," said Kona. "I came on my own."

"You did?" asked Murray. "Stumpy's not with you?"

"No," said Kona.

"Well she's not with *me!*" wailed Murray. "She said she'd go get *you!*"

"WHERE IS SHE?" the two said together.

Kona's heart sank. He looked all around the deathly quiet park.

"Stump!" he called. "Stump!"

"Oh, woe," said Murray, shaking his head. "She said she'd find you and you could help us. Now she's disappeared. Oh, woe."

One of the babies inside the hole began to cry. Another sneezed.

"These kids are freezing," said Murray. He went back inside the hole to wrap them in his wings.

Kona was torn. He had to look for Stumpy, but where had she gone? She had never been to his house, so how did she think she would find him? The fall must have rattled her senses. Kona wanted to keep looking for her, but the babies needed shelter—and quickly. It would be very dangerous for them to be exposed to the cold much longer.

Kona made his decision. He spoke into the hole.

"We have to get you to my house, Murray. You and the babies. Then I'll come back to search for Stumpy."

"*Me* and the babies?" Murray said from within. "Me? I'll be OK."

"I can't get them out of here alone," said Kona.

"Can't you just call a cab or something?"

Kona was thinking hard.

"I've got it," he said. "You can all ride on my back."

"Excuse me?" said Murray. He popped his head out of the hole again.

"It's the only way," Kona insisted. "You can sit on my back and tuck the children inside your wings. It will be like riding a horse."

"Sure, like I've ever ridden a horse," answered

Murray. "We're gonna end up on *Hard Copy*. I know it."

But within minutes, Murray was on Kona's back, humming nervously, the babies tucked under his wings.

Now that Kona had to carry everyone, he was really worried. He had fallen dozens of times on his way to the park, but he couldn't risk any such accidents on the journey home. There was only one thing to do.

"What?" Murray called out. "We're *crawling?* We're going to *crawl?* Gee, maybe we'll get there by September!"

"We'll make it," said Kona. "Just hold tight to those babies."

"Ouch!" Murray yelled. "Ouch! Doesn't Stumpy ever feed these kids?"

It took Kona an hour and a half to make what was usually a ten-minute walk to his house. It was a good thing he was a Labrador retriever. Labradors can withstand very cold temperatures and great pain, and only a dog like Kona could have made the

grueling journey home. In the moonlight of the clearing sky, everything glittered like diamonds, as if all the world had become a jewel, and even as Kona pulled himself across the yards, he was moved and strengthened by the incredible beauty all around him. He might even have forgotten that the others were with him had not Murray yelled "Giddyap!" every five minutes.

R e s c u e a n d R e m o r s e

When Kona finally saw Professor Albert's house again and saw that the front door was still slightly ajar and that the fireplace still glowed and that he was home, he wanted to weep. It was as if he were gazing at heaven itself.

When Kona turned into the yard, Murray knew, too, that they had arrived.

"Yippee!" he yelled.

Kona struggled up the icy steps, then cautiously put his head inside the door. Professor Albert still lay snoring on the sofa.

"Welcome back, dear," Gwendolyn said softly.

Kona walked into the room and gently lay down on the floor. Murray scooped the babies up and hopped off.

"Wow," said Murray. "Look at the size of that television! Did I tell you I love *Jeopardy?*"

Gwendolyn smiled at Kona.

"A remarkable dog," she said.

CHAPTER TEN

The Wanderer

When Professor Albert finally woke up, it was four o'clock in the morning. Gwendolyn was waving her antennae like an inspired conductor; Kona could be heard rattling around down in the basement; some little bits of . . . egg roll? . . . lay on the carpet; and the world outside was nothing but solid, unyielding ice. It was too much for an old biology professor. He refilled Kona's dish, handed Gwendolyn a piece of broccoli, put on an extra pair of socks, and went straight to his bedroom. Professor Albert had never been an amateur when it came to sleeping. Years of standing beside philosophy majors trying to label the insides of frogs had taught him the fine art of turning off his brain whenever he wished. So he turned it off and went back to sleep.

Down in the basement, Kona was trying to settle his houseguests into a giant box of Christmas decorations.

"This is embarrassing," said Kona, plumping a Christmas tree skirt around the babies with a gentle paw. "Ordinarily I'd put you in the guest room—very nice, its own bath—but I don't think we could count on a hearty welcome from Professor Albert. Once a chipmunk wandered in and he chased it for two hours with a colander."

"He cooks Italian?" said Murray.

Kona smiled and turned to leave.

"I hope you find Stumpy," Murray said suddenly, solemnly.

Kona nodded and looked again at the three sleeping children.

The Wanderer

"Now that the professor is in his bedroom, I'll be able to go to the park again," Kona said. "I'll toss down a bag of marshmallows before I go. Then I'll get some real food for you when I get back."

"Marshmallows are real food," said Murray, perking up.

"Wish me luck, Murray," Kona said, quickly going up the stairs.

It was a painful run back to the park. Kona's cuts stung badly in the cold. The pads of his feet hurt from the ice's abrasion. And his entire body ached.

But the dog made it back to the park, and this time more quickly. He was afraid Stumpy might be

The Wanderer

injured and hurting somewhere. There was no time to waste thinking of his own bumps and bruises.

A few of the animals in Gooseberry Park had begun to emerge from the wreckage. They wandered slowly in the moonlight. A large black crow flew low overhead, surveying the sight.

"Have you seen a little red squirrel?" Kona called to the crow.

"A girl?" asked the crow.

"No, no. A squirrel. A little red one." Kona waited as the crow landed beside him.

"A squirrel, you say?" asked the crow.

"Yes," said Kona.

"Red?"

"Yes."

"About this big?" asked the crow, opening his wings.

"Yes, yes!" Kona cried excitedly.

"No," the crow said.

"No?" repeated Kona.

The crow spread his enormous wings and left.

"Gwendolyn was right," Kona muttered to himself as the bird disappeared. "Crows really *are* smart alecks."

Kona sniffed all around the fallen pin oak. It was difficult to catch a good scent, with the ground so frozen and so much of Stumpy's home scattered.

A possum limped past. Her ear was bleeding.

"I've lost my boy!" she said to Kona. "Have you seen my boy?"

"No. I'm sorry," Kona replied with concern.

"Mama!" a voice cried out from a nearby spruce.

The possum gasped. "He's there! I'm coming, dear, I'm coming!"

Kona smiled and watched as the mother possum made her way across the ice to her son. A small gray shape slipped down the trunk of the spruce and leaped onto her back.

Watching them leave, Kona felt a heavy sadness.

Turning, he called, "Stumpy! Stumpy!"

"Whoo?" a voice asked from the branches of a fallen walnut tree. "Whoo?" it asked again.

Kona saw two large yellow eyes peering at him through the branches.

"Stumpy, the little red squirrel," Kona answered. "Do you know her?"

The owl lifted himself up and flew nearer Kona.

"I certainly do," said the owl. "She has those

babies with the strange names. What are they . . . Up? Down?"

"Top and Bottom," Kona answered. "And Sparrow, the little girl."

"Oh yes, lovely children." The owl suddenly winced with pain.

"Are you all right?" Kona asked in alarm.

"Thank you, yes. Just a twist in the neck from the fall. I was eating dinner when my tree went down. Paying no attention whatever. It hit before I knew what was happening."

"Did you see Stumpy? Have you seen her since the storm?"

"I heard her," the owl said.

"Heard her? Where? When?"

"I am not certain when," said the owl. "The evening is a bit of a blur, you know. But I heard her. She was saying, 'I have to find Paradise Lane.'"

"Oh, my goodness!" exclaimed Kona. "She's looking for me, and she's completely confused! Paradise Lane is where I was born, not where I live now! My home is on Miller Street!"

The Wanderer

"Oh, my," said the owl. "That is nowhere near Paradise Lane."

"I know, I know!" cried the dog. "If she's headed to Paradise Lane, she'll never find me! And how will I ever find her?"

The owl began to shake his head. This took a while, of course. When an owl shakes his head, he first must turn it very, very slowly to the far, far left.

He must then turn it very, very slowly to the far, far right. Kona was amazed as he watched.

The owl winced again.

"Your neck," said Kona.

"Yes," said the owl.

"But why did you shake your head?" asked Kona.

"Because you will not be able to find her," said the owl.

"But I have to!"

"She is wandering, my boy, and no one can find a wanderer. The wanderer must first find you."

Kona sighed with frustration.

"Stumpy isn't very smart. She doesn't even know what a television is."

"A what?" asked the owl.

"Never mind," Kona said glumly. "My feet are frozen and there are three babies and a bat in the Christmas ornaments, and then Professor Albert's marshmallows—"

"Snap out of it, son!" the owl grumbled. "Go on home now. You're babbling."

Kona turned to go back home.

The Wanderer

"And where are all of her yogurt cups?" he said. "And the rubber bands . . . Did Murray say he's *Italian?*"

The owl sat and stared as the large weary Labrador mumbled and slipped his way across the ice, heading back to his home on Miller Street, wishing it were Paradise.

CHAPTER ELEVEN

Guests

Later that morning Murray rubbed his eyes, stretched his wings, and gave a giant yawn. Top, Bottom, and Sparrow were all sleeping soundly against him. And Kona was coming down the stairs.

Murray grinned and waved at the dog.

"Say, Kona! What's for breakfast?"

"Breakfast?" said the dog. "You want breakfast?"

Murray nodded.

"Murray, when I got back from Gooseberry Park this morning at six, you ate a whole bag of Fritos, a box of Ritz crackers, a sixteen-ounce package of provolone cheese, and an orange."

"I ate an orange?" Murray asked.

"It's only ten. How in the world can you still be hungry?" said the dog.

"I *never* eat oranges," Murray said.

"How can you even move?" Kona asked.

"They make me break out," said the bat.

Murray looked down at the pile of sleeping babies.

"Hi, gang," he said. "Want a Pop-Tart?"

"Just wait here," said Kona. "I'll bring something down soon. The pudding cup seemed to be all right for the babies last night, so I'll try to steal another one for them. But you have to stay here and keep quiet, Murray. We can't let Professor Albert find you."

"Sure," answered Murray cheerfully. "No problem. But . . . what are my chances of getting a Mars bar?"

"Just *stay,*" said Kona, disappearing back up the stairs.

Guests

Murray sighed. He looked all around the basement. Pipes. Wires. What to do?

Suddenly the sound of a television show came drifting down.

"*Jeopardy!*" cried Murray. "My favorite!"

He jumped out of the box, ready to dash upstairs. Then he remembered Kona's instruction: *Stay.*

Murray walked in circles around and around the box, hearing the familiar theme song float down from above.

"Oh-oh-oh-oh-oh-oh," said Murray, trying hard to stay. Trying *really* hard to stay.

"But Alex Trebek is my idol!" he wailed. And, *flum-flum-flum,* he was on his way.

The basement steps led to the kitchen. Murray flew in and, hiding inside a china cabinet, poked his head out and looked toward the living room. Professor Albert was watching television and eating a Danish. Kona sat beside him, looking rather impatient and glancing often toward the basement. Kona didn't see Murray in the cabinet.

"And now we'll begin our round of Double Jeopardy," said Alex Trebek.

Guests

Murray sighed with pleasure and settled down to watch.

Soon, however, the sight and smell of Professor Albert's Danish was just too much for the tiny bat. He was hungry. He needed breakfast.

Murray's nose went up in the air, sniffing, sniffing.

"Hmmm," said the little bat to himself. "Now where would a professor keep a Danish?"

He flew to the top of the cabinet and looked out over the confusion of Professor Albert's kitchen counters.

"A bottle of vitamin C. Bottle of vitamin A. Bottle of vitamin E. Gee, I'm watering at the mouth." His eyes searched a different counter.

"Wheat germ. Olive oil. Soybean curd—oh, *gross!* Maple granola. Oreos. Lima beans . . . OREOS!"

Murray jumped so hard he hit his head on the ceiling. *Thump!*

In the living room Kona pricked up his ears. The dog looked toward the kitchen and saw Murray hopping up and down on top of the china cabinet, waving to him and pointing to something below. Kona nearly fainted. He shook his head fiercely at Murray.

The bat mouthed some words to him. "Creamy center" was all Kona could make out.

The Labrador frowned and firmly shook his head again. He had to wait for Professor Albert to take a morning nap before carrying any more food to the basement. The professor would likely be home all day, with the ice outside still so thick. They were lucky even to have the electricity back on.

And Murray was supposed to be staying in the basement, but there he was, bouncing like a ball on the china cabinet.

Murray *had* to behave. Kona vigorously shook his head at the bat again.

"A flea, Kona?" the professor asked, putting down his Danish and rubbing Kona's ears.

"No, just a *pest,*" the Labrador said to himself.

Back in the kitchen, Murray threw up his wings in exasperation.

"A whole bag of Oreos in the kitchen, and the dog only wants his ears scratched. Domestic animals—who can figure 'em?"

Flum. Murray dropped down to the kitchen counter.

Just then Professor Albert rose and said something about needing some butter.

"Uh-oh," said Murray, who was just getting to his first creamy center.

Professor Albert started for the kitchen.

"Double uh-oh!" Murray said again, stuffing the Oreo in his mouth and looking for a place to hide.

The professor took a few more steps toward the kitchen. But before he could get there—

CRASH!

"What?!" The professor spun around.

On the living room floor Professor Albert's Chinese ginger jar lamp lay in a hundred pieces. Kona sat very still and wagged his tail. Just a bit.

Murray seized his opportunity. The cookie still in his mouth, he grabbed two more with his feet and flew down the basement steps.

Back in the living room, Professor Albert was saying that he didn't understand how a lamp could just knock itself off a table and why did he keep thinking he heard a bird in the house and, really, weren't the past twenty-four hours the strangest anyone had ever seen?

Kona, glancing over at the sleeping Gwendolyn, tried to wipe the guilty look off his face. He could not have agreed more with the old professor.

CHAPTER TWELVE

Food and Conversation

For the next few days while Kona and Gwendolyn tried to figure out how to find Stumpy, bags of nacho chips, boxes of after dinner mints, jars of crunchy peanut butter, and the occasional chocolate bar with almonds kept disappearing mysteriously from the kitchen. Poor Professor Albert. He would stand in front of the refrigerator or in front of the pantry, scratching his head in confusion. He would tell himself that he was *not* getting senile, that he just *thought* he'd bought that bag of chips or that jar of peanut butter. No cans of lima beans or spinach ever disappeared. It was as if some force in the universe wanted Professor Albert to eat only healthy things. And he still couldn't figure out why Kona was so nervous every time they watched *Jeopardy.* Things certainly had seemed odd since that ice storm.

But Professor Albert's problems were nothing compared to Kona's. The dog was constantly going through the house picking up empty potato chip bags or candy wrappers. If Professor Albert found these, he would surely think that Kona was the one taking his food. And Kona certainly was *not* the one.

"You have to clean up after yourself, Murray," Kona would say to the bat.

"Oh, sorry, Kona," Murray would answer. "But I was watching *Days of Our Lives* through the heat vent and I was so upset about Daniel and Laura that I forgot those Milky Way wrappers. Daniel is such a rat!"

Still, in spite of his hectic life and his worries about Stumpy, Kona was enjoying having Murray and the babies at his house. And late night was the best time of all.

Food and Conversation

Long after Professor Albert had gone off to bed—complaining again that he just couldn't understand where an entire bag of Chips Ahoy could disappear to and speculating that another of those pesky chipmunks was sneaking in—Kona, finally able to relax, would softly pad over to Gwendolyn's bowl, pick her up gently in his mouth, and the two would sneak down into the basement.

Murray, being nocturnal, was always wide awake and usually swinging by his feet somewhere. When Kona and Gwendolyn appeared, he would do a little somersault and land with his wings outspread.

"Ta-da!" he'd sing. "So, who's got the Pepsi?"

Top, Bottom, and Sparrow would lift their little heads and look up from the box at Gwendolyn.

"Oh dear, oh dear! Such pretty babies!" the crab would fuss. "Such chubby little legs! And is that a tooth you have, Mister Bottom?" Gwendolyn's antennae moved wildly in the air.

Kona beamed with joy. He loved the babies, too.

Then the friends would all gather in and around the box in the quiet night. Murray told vampire

Food and Conversation

jokes ("Why do vampires brush their teeth in the morning?" "To fight bat breath!"); Gwendolyn read everyone's palm; and Kona told them again the story of his icy journey to Gooseberry Park. They all loved to hear it.

When Kona told them about the cat who strolled

Food and Conversation

across the Oldsmobile, Murray said, "I know that cat. His name is Conroy. He eats Chinese, too. Plus French. Italian. Canadian. Anybody will do!" The bat cracked up over his joke.

And at times they were serious and wistful.

"Do you think she'll find us?" Kona asked.

"I am certain of it, dear," Gwendolyn answered. "I can feel it in my bones."

"You have bones?" Murray asked the crab.

"Figure of speech, Murray," said Kona. "Figure of speech."

And after an hour or two of good food and conversation, Kona began to yawn.

"How can you be sleepy?" Murray asked. "It's only three o'clock."

"Even I am a bit drowsy," Gwendolyn said, smiling at the bat. "I think it may be due to all of this lovely food you provided." She gestured to the graham crackers, the raisin bread, the banana chips scattered about.

"We didn't even get to the pretzels and bean dip yet," said Murray.

Food and Conversation

Kona and Gwendolyn bade their friend good night, kissed the babies, and returned quietly upstairs. Kona eased Gwendolyn down into her bowl, then looked at her through the glass. Each night he said the same thing: "I hope Stumpy finds us."

And each night Gwendolyn's answer was the same: "She will."

CHAPTER THIRTEEN

The Weasel

It was several days after the ice storm before Professor Albert took Kona to Gooseberry Park again. First they had to wait for warmer air to blow in and the ice to melt. Then they had to wait for park crews to remove the devastation of fallen trees. The sound of chain saws filled the air, leaving everyone in Professor Albert's house with a heavy heart. Particularly Kona. He thought of Stumpy's cozy nest

The Weasel

destroyed, all her treasures scattered and gone. And he wondered if he really would ever see her again.

Finally Professor Albert resumed his walks to the park, and Kona was mightily relieved, for he had hopes of hearing news there of Stumpy. With the warmer weather, many animals would be out. Someone was bound to know something.

When he arrived at Gooseberry Park, Kona could not help his hopes sinking a little. Nearly every tree had suffered some injury, and many had not survived at all. Large piles of sawed trunks and branches lay everywhere. The remains of Stumpy's beautiful pin oak were among them.

Still, Kona could sense in the air a spirit of renewal around him. The animals were stirring. There was life. There was hope.

While Professor Albert read a book on clams, Kona took off to look for clues to Stumpy's whereabouts. He stopped to chat with a chipmunk who had just awakened from hibernation and was still a little groggy.

"Are you acquainted with a squirrel named Stumpy?" Kona asked.

86

The chipmunk yawned. "Whose cabbage was it?" he said.

Kona sighed and moved on.

Then Kona met a mallard duck who said that no, he didn't know what had become of Stumpy, but that the weasels on the West Side were bound to know something. All weasels lived for gossip and sensational events. And if one weasel knew something, *all* weasels knew it.

Kona thanked the mallard and headed across the park.

Once he arrived on the West Side, it didn't take Kona long to find a weasel. He simply stood on a tree stump and said as loudly as he could, "What a *strange story!*" And sure enough, from behind a broken maple a weasel popped out his head.

The weasel ran over to Kona, sniffing the air.

"What's strange?" the weasel asked. "What? What?"

"It's about that squirrel who lost her babies over on the East Side."

"Yeah, I heard about that squirrel," answered the weasel. "So what?"

The Weasel

"Well," Kona replied confidentially, "I hear that a dog on Miller Street . . . Do you know Miller Street?"

"Yeah, I know it! I know it! Go on!" said the weasel.

"Well," Kona continued, "a dog on Miller Street has some treasure that belongs to that squirrel, but he can't find her anywhere. And he actually wants to give the treasure *back*. Now, isn't that strange?"

"The dog lives on Miller Street, you say?" asked the weasel.

"Right," said Kona, thinking as fast as he could. "And I hear he's planning to put a sign on his house tomorrow night. So the squirrel can find him."

The Weasel

"What kind of sign?" asked the weasel. "Like, WELCOME SQUIRREL or something?"

"No. I hear that it's going to be a sign only the squirrel will know. A secret sign," Kona answered. "Imagine. Leading straight to treasure!"

"You sure it's Miller Street?" the weasel, who was always interested in treasure, asked.

"Oh yes," said Kona. "Tomorrow night. A sign for the squirrel on Miller Street. I'm positive."

"So, do you know what the sign is?" asked the weasel, his sharp little nose twitching.

"No," said Kona. "Afraid not."

"Then what good are you?" the weasel sneered. And he ran off to find another weasel who might know about a sign for a squirrel on Miller Street.

The Weasel

With a sigh of relief, Kona watched the weasel run away. Then the dog turned and hurried back to Professor Albert and home, for he had a very important task ahead of him now.

Before tomorrow night, he had to think of a *sign*.

CHAPTER FOURTEEN

A Brilliant Idea

"Top won't eat his pudding and Bottom keeps trying to climb out of the box and Sparrow has the hiccups and I'm going CRAZY!" Murray yelled as Kona and Gwendolyn came into the basement that evening. "I want a night off!"

Gwendolyn clicked her claws in sympathy.

"Oh yes. Being a young mother can be so difficult at times."

A Brilliant Idea

"It sure can," agreed Murray. "And what I need is— Wait a minute! I'm not a young mother! I'm a bat!"

Gwendolyn laughed.

"Of course you are, dear."

"Well," said Murray, "truth is, I think these kids believe I *am* their mother. I mean, I'm always the one who's got the pudding. I'm always the one who rides horsey. I'm always the one going CRAZY!" The bat threw up his wings in exasperation.

"Well, tonight I hope you're the one who gets an idea," said Kona, settling Gwendolyn on top of a plastic Santa.

A Brilliant Idea

"An idea?" said Gwendolyn and Murray together.

And Kona told them about his conversation with the weasel in the park.

"The news about the sign on Miller Street will be all over town by morning," said Kona, "once that weasel starts passing it around. And Stumpy, wherever she is, is bound to hear it. I know she'll come to Miller Street tomorrow night. So we have to give her a sign, a sign that tells her this is Professor Albert's house. That we're *here*. It's our only chance, because goodness knows we'll never find *her*."

"Let's think aloud," said Gwendolyn, ever ready to get down to business. "Now, what do we know about little Stumpy that might give us some idea for a sign?"

"She's a mother," said Kona.

"She likes egg rolls," said Murray.

"She doesn't understand what a television is," said Kona.

"She collects things," said Murray.

"The collection!" said Gwendolyn. "Kona dear, is there anything from her collection we could use to signal her to this house?"

A Brilliant Idea

Kona thought of the terrible sight of the shattered pin oak in Gooseberry Park. The crews with chain saws. The remains of the cozy nest.

"No," he said sadly. "I don't think there is anything at all left of Stumpy's collection. I didn't see a single ice-cream stick or gum wrapper when I went back with Professor Albert. Besides, how would she see such a small thing at night?

"She will be so upset," continued Kona, "losing all her treasure. Even more upset than when she lost that wonderful watch."

"What watch?" asked Murray.

"A glow-in-the-dark watch Stumpy found on a picnic table," explained Kona. "She loved it. But somebody stole it."

"Wow, it really glowed in the dark?" asked the bat.

"Yes, it—"

"That's it!" cried Gwendolyn.

"What?" Kona and Murray jumped at the same time.

"We have to find that watch," answered the crab.

A Brilliant Idea

"The watch that glows. The watch that glows *in the dark*. If we put it on the roof, Stumpy will see it glowing. And she'll know it's the sign!"

"But, Gwendolyn," said Kona, "how will we ever find that watch? Stumpy searched and searched and she never found it. We haven't a clue. We haven't a lead. We haven't a—"

"Weasel," finished Gwendolyn.

"A what?" asked Kona.

"We haven't a weasel," said the crab, "and we need one. As you discovered, dear, the weasels know everything. Find a weasel and you'll find the watch. Find the watch and you'll find Stumpy."

"Find me a hamburger," said Murray, "and I'll find fries."

Kona smiled thankfully at Gwendolyn. A good friend was good to have. But an old and *wise* friend was even better.

Things were looking up.

CHAPTER FIFTEEN

Yet Another Muckraker

There are muckrakers everywhere, mucking about in everyone's business, and Gooseberry Park certainly had its fair share. Especially on the West Side. It didn't take Kona long to find another weasel. And this time Kona had an advantage: this time Kona had *Murray*.

As Professor Albert and Kona walked toward the park the following morning, the little silver-and-black bat zipped around in the sky, just above their heads. Occasionally the bat faked a dive-bomb straight for the big dog's nose, which caused Kona to leap and Professor Albert to shriek.

"What *is* that bat doing, Kona?" Professor Albert cried, waving his arms wildly at the little figure in the sky.

Kona knew exactly what that bat was doing and he knew exactly what a good dog should do in such a case—though he really wasn't in the mood. But he stood tall and barked and barked and barked. Professor Albert was very proud. Murray was hysterical.

However, the mischievous bat did keep a low profile for the rest of the walk. Then once Professor Albert was settled and reading (this time it was snails), Murray flew down to join Kona, who was heading for the West Side.

"Very funny, Murray," said Kona as he raced across the park.

"You thought so, too?" called the bat from the air. "Oh, I was dying! Dying!"

Kona gave a huff of disapproval and ran on.

Yet Another Muckraker

When they reached the infamous west side of Gooseberry Park, Murray did an *Oh-that's-just-awful* routine, and sure enough, a weasel popped up out of nowhere.

"Something going on?" he said in a low voice.

"There certainly is, if you must know," answered the little bat, perching on a bush near Kona's head. "This dog here says he knows the identity of a thief, a thief who stole a very valuable piece of jewelry from a friend of mine. And do you know that this dog wants me to *pay* him for the name of the thief? Now, is that awful or what?"

The weasel narrowed his weasely eyes (a common response among weasels) and said to Kona, "That so?"

"A dog's got to make a living," said Kona. The weasel nodded, looking shrewdly at the dog.

"What makes you think you know who the thief is?" the weasel asked Kona.

"None of your business," said the dog.

"What's the piece of jewelry anyway?" asked the weasel.

"None of your business again," said the dog.

"It's a glow-in-the-dark watch!" said Murray.

The weasel's eyes lit up. At once Kona could see that the weasel knew who had the watch! (Kona finally believed it: weasels knew *everything*.) Now all Kona and Murray had to do was bait him.

"What's the dog's price?" the weasel hissed toward Murray.

"Egg rolls," answered the bat.

"Egg rolls?" repeated the weasel. "How many egg rolls?"

"Six of 'em, can you believe it?" answered the bat. "I told him only three, but *no-o-o-o,* he wants six. No wonder he's so fat."

The little bat grinned as Kona gave him a sharp look.

"Six, huh?" said the weasel, thinking things over. He moved closer to where the bat perched and said quietly, "Suppose I give you the information you want and you give me five egg rolls?"

"Five?" cried the bat. "Highway robbery!"

The weasel smiled.

Yet Another Muckraker

"You won't get the information anywhere else for less," he said.

"Oh yeah? Just watch me!" The little bat lifted to fly away.

"Three!" shouted the weasel. "Three egg rolls." The thought had him drooling.

Murray perched again.

"Two," he said. "I bring two, and you tell me who's got the watch."

The weasel knew Murray had him. Any weasel in the park would probably sell the name for just one egg roll. Weasels had no scruples. And they were all so sick of eating mice.

"Deal!" hissed the weasel.

"Deal!" shouted Murray, and off he flew to the Chinese Dumpster. Kona, pretending to be angry at losing six egg rolls, glared at the weasel and trotted away (actually, back to the South Side, where he would wait for Murray's return).

The old professor had fallen asleep (snails can be so tedious) by the time Murray finally came barreling back to Kona through the trees. Murray landed on the professor's head.

Yet Another Muckraker

"Murray!" Kona jumped up. "Be careful!"

"Don't worry," said the bat. "I have very delicate little feet. He can't feel a thing."

"Who has the watch?" Kona asked.

"First let me say that if I ever see another weasel again it will be too soon."

"Who has it?"

"I'm ashamed to tell you," said the bat, dropping his head.

Yet Another Muckraker

"Who?" said Kona.

"It's a disgrace," said the bat.

"Who?" said Kona.

"And I want you to know that every family has its black sheep," said the bat. "And I'm not it."

"WHO, Murray, WHO?" cried the dog.

"My big fat cousin Ralph," answered the bat.

"What? Your cousin?" Kona asked. "Your *cousin* stole Stumpy's watch?"

"Ralph the Mouth, we call him. Eats *all* the time. If you think I'm bad, you should meet Ralph."

"But why did he steal Stumpy's watch?" asked Kona.

"Oh, it's so tacky. *Tacky!*" said Murray.

"Why?"

"The light attracts moths," Murray answered. "Ralph—who lives on the roof of Malley's Department Store, by the way—Ralph just sits there on the roof with the watch glowing every night and his mouth wide open. Isn't that disgusting? I can't understand who'd want a moth anyway, with all the Dumpsters in the world. Why, I've found whole

Yet Another Muckraker

pepperoni pizzas. Chicken nuggets. French toast with syrup!"

"Murray," said Kona impatiently, "forget Ralph's bad taste. You have to get that watch."

Murray sighed.

"Boy, is my aunt Olive going to be mad at me."

"Aunt Olive?"

"Ralph's mother. She'll never speak to me again if I take that watch. She probably thinks he won it in a poker game."

"I'll never speak to you again if you *don't* take it," said Kona.

"No more Thanksgiving dinners at Aunt Olive's house," said Murray, shaking his head sadly.

"You have to," Kona said sternly.

"No more beet casseroles."

"You have to do it, Murray."

"No more mashed turnips."

"Murray, I'm not kidding."

"No more fried liver— Hey, wait a minute! I *hate* all that stuff! Yuck! Ack! Yes, oh *yes,* I'll get that watch. I will *love* getting that watch! Just watch me!

Yet Another Muckraker

Ha, ha, get it?" Murray danced on Professor Albert's head. The old professor mumbled and shifted.

"Hurry, Murray," Kona urged. "We need that watch by tonight. Stumpy will be running through the trees on Miller Street all evening, I'm sure of it. We need that watch."

"You've got it," said Murray. "By supper time. By the way, is this lasagna night?"

"Hurry!" Kona implored.

"I'm off," the little bat said, leaping from the professor's head. "Save me some garlic bread, Kona!"

Away the bat flew, a tiny speck in the sky. Kona watched him until he was out of sight.

"We've almost found you, Stump," the good dog whispered. "Almost."

CHAPTER SIXTEEN

The Sign

Murray arrived with the watch still in time for lasagna. He zipped down the chimney, popped out into the living room, and plunked the precious object at the feet of Kona, who was sleeping beneath Gwendolyn's bowl. Professor Albert had gone out to play bingo.

"Wonderful job, dear!" Gwendolyn applauded with her claws.

Kona jumped to his feet at the sound of her voice.

"It's here? We have it?" he asked.

The Sign

"Ta-da!" Murray pointed to the watch on the floor.

The dog took one look and nearly burst into tears. But he knew that would be a very undoglike thing to do.

"Murray," Kona said, "after dinner you'll have to take the watch up to the roof and stay there for the rest of the night. Until Stumpy finds you."

"Right-o," said Murray. "I could use some fresh air anyway. You wouldn't believe my cousin Ralph's apartment. All those pieces of moth. Yuck."

"Did you have any trouble, dear?" asked Gwendolyn.

"Nah," said Murray. "Ralph was napping—his *second* favorite hobby. Besides, I've been sneaking things out of places all my life."

"If Stumpy shows up tonight, you'll have more sneaking to do," said Kona. "Sneaking her *in.*"

"A snap," said Murray. "This house is full of holes."

"Wake me up, dear, if I'm sleeping," said Gwendolyn.

The Sign

"Me, too," said Kona.

"I'll never understand animals who sleep at night," Murray said, shaking his head. "They miss all the good stuff."

After he gobbled down a huge plate of lasagna and garlic bread, the little bat picked up the watch and flew out to the roof to wait for Stumpy.

Inside the house the night seemed endless. The professor came back home and went to bed. Kona and Gwendolyn went down and tended to the sleeping babies awhile, then returned upstairs. They were restless, constantly listening for footsteps on the roof, forever looking out the window.

"What time is it, dear?" Gwendolyn asked.

"The news is over; Professor Albert's in bed. It must be past midnight."

"Poor little Stumpy," said Gwendolyn. "All alone out there, worried so for her children. Natural disasters are hard on families."

"Especially families that live in trees," added Kona.

The old crab nodded.

The Sign

The two friends talked and talked and waited and waited.

Up on the roof Murray was keeping himself occupied by making lists in his head. First he listed things that were green: limes, olives, Christmas trees, Kermit the Frog. He listed yellow things: corn, sunflowers, lemons, Big Bird. Blue things: swimming pools, berries, the sky, Cookie Monster. (Murray had watched a lot of *Sesame Street* in Professor Albert's house.) He had gone through a purple list, an orange list, a red list, and a white list, and was just beginning a striped list when he heard someone in the trees whisper his name.

"Murray?"

The little bat jumped. For a second he forgot about Stumpy and thought his cousin Ralph had found him.

"Nope!" he said.

"Murray, it *is* you!" A little shadow with a big fluffy tail leaped from way up in the trees and landed on the roof with a thump. Murray knew that tail.

The Sign

"Stumpy! Stumpy!" He jumped up and down, flapping his wings. "Good golly, Miss Molly!"

The little red squirrel scurried across the roof and into the light of the watch. Tears were streaming down her face, which made tears stream down Murray's face, and the two stood there on the roof together, hugging and crying.

"My babies?" sobbed Stumpy.

"Fat and sassy!" sobbed Murray.

"Kona?" the little squirrel cried.

"Fat and bossy!" Murray cried harder.

The Sign

Stumpy laughed and began to wipe away Murray's tears.

"And you, Murray?" she asked gently.

"Just *fat!*" answered the little bat with a teary grin. "And I bet I have the *worst* garlic breath."

Murray sneaked Stumpy through a crack in the house's foundation, and the little mother ran straight across the basement to where her babies lay sleeping. She jumped into the box and picked up all three at once, holding them tight and kissing their little red heads. The children were drowsy, half-asleep. But they seemed to recognize their lost mother, for they held tight to her with their tiny paws. Murray thought he might start bawling again.

The Sign

"Where are Kona and Gwendolyn?" Stumpy asked over her children's sleeping heads.

"I forgot!" cried Murray. "I was supposed to tell them first thing!"

Murray flew up the basement steps and did a snappy tap dance across the living room floor.

Kona raised his big head. He looked at Murray.

"Is she here?" Kona asked anxiously.

With a big grin, Murray nodded excitedly and pointed toward the basement.

"Stump!" Kona called. He picked up Gwendolyn—whose antennae flew at the sound of Stumpy's name—and everyone ran for the basement.

The joy the friends shared in their reunion was the best treasure of all to be found on Miller Street that evening. And Kona surprised himself.

He cried.

CHAPTER SEVENTEEN

The Wonders of Technology

Life in Professor Albert's house for the next several days was magical.

Stumpy's wanderings had left her rather thin, so Kona took on the job of fattening her up. Food upstairs continued to disappear at a steady pace. Poor Professor Albert was making trips to the grocery daily. He had decided a sneaky chipmunk definitely was stealing the food, and he contrived several schemes for hiding his groceries. None of them worked, of course. Not with an experienced bat in the house.

Kona had promised himself that once this adventure was over, he would be a perfect dog for Professor Albert forever, to repay him for all the food they'd borrowed and the lamp he'd crashed. He would never pull at the leash. He would never bark at the UPS truck. He would never drip water from his bowl onto the kitchen floor. He would be perfect.

With Murray's help, Kona sneaked boxes of shredded wheat, bags of English muffins, and jars of Spanish peanuts downstairs to his guests. Stumpy's health improved each day, and her children were very happy to have real squirrel milk to grow on again.

Stumpy had told her friends the whole story of her night in the ice storm—how she had left her children in Murray's care, believing she could find Paradise Lane and Kona. She knew Kona would give shelter to them all. But of course, Paradise Lane was the wrong road completely; it was even on the wrong side of town, and for two days Stumpy had wandered

The Wonders of Technology

through all of its yards and trees, looking for a chocolate Labrador.

Then, the third day, on the upper end of Paradise Lane, she saw from high up in a tree a yard where about twenty chocolate Labradors were playing. She thought she was dreaming! She rubbed her eyes hard and looked again. Yes, it was twenty chocolate Labradors, and they all looked like Kona!

Believing she had finally found the house of her friend, Stumpy leaped from the trees, ran across the power lines to the other side of the street, and hopped onto the gate of the yard. She wasn't sure which dog was Kona, they all looked so much alike, so she stood up and yelled as loudly as she could, "KONA, I'M HERE!"

And . . . BARK! BARK! BARK! BARK! BARK! BARK! BARK! Those Labradors chased her right off that gate and into a tree, and they stood under that tree barking at her all day until a woman came home and put them back in the house.

Poor Stumpy. She was very confused, for she did not understand the dogs' unfriendly behavior. They were not at all like Kona. She managed to make her way back to Gooseberry Park, then was stunned when there was no sign of Murray or the children. Her tree was gone. Her family was gone. Her friend was gone. She wandered the town, asking for news of a chocolate dog who might be looking for her. No one could help.

The Wonders of Technology

But then one day, while she still searched, word began to spread about a dog, and a sign for a squirrel on Miller Street. In the morning the rumor traveled through every den in Gooseberry Park (beginning on the West Side, of course). In the afternoon it went above ground and through every tree still standing. By supper time it was out on the street. And at nightfall, when Stumpy wearily asked an old pigeon sitting on the courthouse lawn whether he'd heard of a dog who might be looking for her, the rumor finally hit its target. The old pigeon, who knew every neighborhood in the city, led the little squirrel directly to Miller Street. And the soft green glow of the wonderful watch on the roof of Professor Albert's house led her to Kona.

After staying in the professor's basement for a few days, Stumpy became curious about the way people in houses live. So when Professor Albert was away, Kona would accompany her about the rooms and show her all the wonders of technology she had missed by living in trees.

The Wonders of Technology

Kona showed her the professor's clock radio, his compact disc player, his electric can opener, his VCR with remote control, his toaster, his heating pad, and his refrigerator.

Stumpy was very impressed by all of the food Professor Albert had stored in his refrigerator. Staring at the shelves, she said, "He must have collected all summer long to get this much food put away."

"Oh no," said Kona. "He got most of it just this week."

"Amazing!" Stumpy exclaimed.

But of all Professor Albert's technological wonders, it was his television that Stumpy liked best of all. When her children were asleep and the professor was out, Stumpy would sneak upstairs to see what was on. Because she had always been a very practical squirrel, she liked the PBS station best. She listened to every word of *Wall Street Week* and *The Frugal Gourmet*. But *This Old House* was her favorite, and once, when Professor Albert and Kona were off for a walk, she crept upstairs into the kitchen and fixed the professor's leaky faucet.

It was all quite extraordinary.

The Wonders of Technology

CHAPTER EIGHTEEN

A New Home

After a week or so had passed and Stumpy was strong and healthy enough to be on her own, the friends began talking about finding a new tree for Stumpy and Murray to live in. The two had become like family—especially since Stumpy's children were forever forgetting and calling Murray "Mama"—and it seemed only logical the two should do their house-hunting together.

But Kona, always protective, suggested instead that he do the hunting. Now that the weather was so pleasant, he and Professor Albert were taking walks to the park every day, sometimes two or three times. And Kona had made so many acquaintances in Gooseberry Park since the evening of Stumpy's disappearance that he was sure he could find someone to help him scout things out.

Gwendolyn agreed with the plan.

"Moving makes children nervous," she told Stumpy confidentially. "It's best that Kona find something for you that's all ready and waiting. Then you and the babies can move right in, without too much confusion."

"You're very wise, Gwendolyn," Stumpy told the crab.

"Well . . ." The crab smiled. "One of the benefits of age."

A remarkable fact of nature is that problems almost always get solved just when they are meant to. And those who can help solve the problems almost always show up at just the right time.

Thus it seemed completely logical that as soon as Kona went looking for someone who might help him locate a new house for his friends, he ran into

Conroy, the famous cat. Kona did not know it yet, but running into Conroy was a stroke of good fortune.

"Hey, it's the skating dog," the cat said with a grin, scratching his back against a knobby tree stump.

Kona blushed with embarrassment.

"No, it's cool," assured the cat. "Word of your heroics got around. Even I was impressed."

"Thank you," Kona said gladly.

"So, what's happening?" asked the cat.

And Kona explained what he was searching for.

"You need a tip on a good piece of real estate?" Conroy asked.

Kona nodded.

"You found the right man, my friend." The cat rolled onto his back. "I heard about a place just yesterday," he continued, scratching his back against the grass. "Nice little joint. South Side. Some starlings moved out and went to Florida because of Granny's arthritis."

"How do you know?" asked Kona.

A New Home

"They were always pecking at my head," Conroy answered. "Lovely family," he said sarcastically. "Just hated to see 'em go! You'd better hustle, though. Good trees are scarce since the storm. It won't stay empty for long."

"Gosh," said Kona, turning to go. "I've got to get my friends in there. Today!"

The dog started running.

"Thanks, Conroy!" he called back.

The cat took a deep bow and strolled on.

Kona practically dragged Professor Albert all the

A New Home

The professor kept muttering something about how he should have bought a guinea pig instead of a Labrador. But Kona knew he didn't mean it.

Once they were home, Kona sneaked down to the basement and told Stumpy and Murray the time had come. It was moving day.

"Really?" Stumpy asked.

"Does that mean I'll miss pork chop night?" asked Murray.

Within minutes they were set to go.

"Murray," said Kona, "Stumpy and the kids will ride on my back."

"Right," said the bat, hopping around and testing his wings.

"And you have to fly," said Kona.

"Gee," the bat said, looking at Kona in exasperation, "thanks for helping me figure that out."

"But first you have to be bait," said Kona.

"Excuse me?" said Murray. "Don't you mean *bat?*"

A New Home

"No. *Bait.* You have to go upstairs and flap around the living room," Kona explained, "to make Professor Albert open all the doors and windows. Then you have to get him to chase you into the bedroom so I can get us out the front door."

The bat grinned. "This sounds like fun!"

"Just don't get clobbered," Kona said.

"No problem!"

The dog, with the squirrels on his back, stood ready at the bottom of the steps.

"OK, Murray—GO!" he yelled.

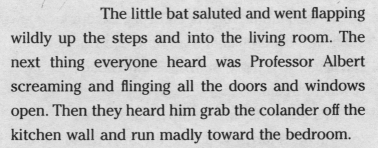

The little bat saluted and went flapping wildly up the steps and into the living room. The next thing everyone heard was Professor Albert screaming and flinging all the doors and windows open. Then they heard him grab the colander off the kitchen wall and run madly toward the bedroom.

"Let's go!" cried Kona. He raced up the steps and straight out the front door. As they were leaving,

A New Home

Stumpy and the babies waved cheerfully to Gwendolyn, who from her bowl hailed them with a claw.

Kona galloped down the sidewalk as the squirrels hung on and cheered. He loved being a hero again.

They made it to the south side of Gooseberry Park, then after a few queries they found the tree where the starlings had been living. Except for a few sunflower seed hulls and a half-eaten hot dog bun, the place was empty. And, like Conroy had promised, it was a dream.

"It's a split-level!" Stumpy called down to Kona in delight. "Murray can take the upper and we can take the lower! And it's in a sugar maple! Just like the one I was born in!"

A New Home

Kona looked up and smiled. He waited while Stumpy and her children wandered the rooms. Stumpy poked her head out of a hole.

"And there's plenty of room for treasure!" she called.

Kona sighed with pleasure.

While the dog was imagining all the new treasure Stumpy would be collecting, suddenly Murray came careening through the trees. He grabbed on to a

branch of the maple, whirled and bounced, then hung there, bobbing like a spring.

"Wow!" he cried.

"Are you all right?" Kona called.

"I'm all right," said the little bat, brushing himself off. "But it's sure too bad about that television!"

CHAPTER NINETEEN

The Wonderful Watch

By the middle of the summer, Professor Albert had replaced the thirty-inch television he had cracked with a flying colander, and Kona had taught Bottom to catch a tiny Frisbee in his mouth. Sparrow and Top had their mother's interests: they collected things, and they spent hours down on the riverbank seeing what people might have thrown out that day. Stumpy spent her time as usual: housekeeping

The Wonderful Watch

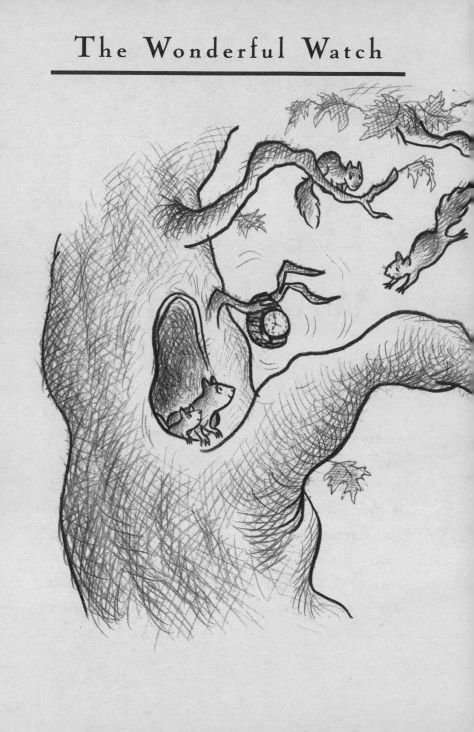

The Wonderful Watch

(well, a little); food collecting (she didn't trust Murray's hand-to-mouth existence); and admiring all the new treasures her children were bringing home.

Beside the front door of Stumpy and Murray's dear home hung the wonderful and famous glow-in-the-dark watch. It cast its green heavenly light all around, and this time every animal in the park seemed respectful of the halo. Even Ralph.

When Stumpy's children were old enough to stay out at night with friends, Stumpy would point to a number on the watch's face.

"Be home by this time," she would say like a good mother. And the children were.

And though Murray continued to bump his way through Gooseberry Park on his forays out for egg rolls or curly fries, he never ever bumped into his own tree again. From wherever he was, the glow of the watch led him safely back.

And across the way, on Miller Street, in Professor Albert's peaceful house . . .

The Wonderful Watch

Late at night Kona and Gwendolyn would sit together and talk of all the wonderful adventures they had had. They loved retelling their favorite Murray stories. They loved chatting about the children. And from time to time, Kona had to recount yet again his magnificent journey across the ice.

The two old friends would talk through the deep night, and now and then they would look over to the window, across the tops of the houses, and up into the familiar trees. There, in the darkness, they could see a lovely green radiance, a welcoming light . . . a treasure in Gooseberry Park.

ABOUT THE AUTHOR

Cynthia Rylant is the acclaimed author of more than fifty books for young people, including her novel *Missing May*, which received the Newbery Medal in 1993. Her other titles include *The Dreamer*, *I Had Seen Castles*, *Something Permanent*, *When I Was Young in the Mountains*, *When the Relatives Came*, *A Fine White Dust*, *The Bookshop Dog*, *Whales*, and the Poppleton books. She lives in Eugene, Oregon.

ABOUT THE ILLUSTRATOR

New York artist Arthur Howard is the illustrator of Cynthia Rylant's Mr. Putter and Tabby series, as well as many humor books for adults. He is also an actor who has appeared in the Children's Television Workshop production *Square One Television*.